Kipper

Other Kipper Books

Kipper's Toybox

Kipper's Birthday

Kipper's Snowy Day

Where, Oh Where, Is Kipper's Bear?

Kipper's Book of Colors

Kipper's Book of Numbers

Kipper's Book of Opposites

Kipper's Book of Weather

Little Kippers

Arnold

Honk!

Sandcastle

Splosh!

Requests for permission to make copies of any part of the work should be mailed to:
Permissions Department, Harcourt Brace & Company,
6277 Sea Harbor Drive, Orlando, Florida 32887-6777.

First published in Great Britain in 1991 by Hodder Children's Books

First Red Wagon Books edition 1999

Red Wagon Books is a registered trademark of Harcourt Brace & Company.

Library of Congress Cataloging-in-Publication Data
Inkpen, Mick.
Kipper/Mick Inkpen.
p. cm.
"Red Wagon Books."
Summary: Tired of his old blanket and basket, Kipper the dog searches
among the animals outside for a new place to sleep.
ISBN 0-15-202294-5
[1. Dogs—Fiction. 2. Animals—Fiction.] I. Title.
PZ7.I564Ki 1999
[E]—dc21 99-6093

E F

Printed in Hong Kong

Kipper

Mick Inkpen

Red Wagon Books

Harcourt Brace & Company

San Diego   New York   London

Kipper was in the mood for tidying his basket.

"You are falling apart!" he said to his rabbit.

"You are chewed and you are soggy!" he said to his ball and his bone.

"And you are DISGUSTING!" he said to his smelly old blanket.

Out they went.
"That's better!" said Kipper.

But it was not better. Now his basket was uncomfortable.

He twisted and he turned. He wiggled and he wriggled. But it was no good. He could not get comfortable.

"Silly basket!" said Kipper . . .

. . . and he went outside.

Outside there were two ducks.
They looked very comfortable
standing on one leg.

   "That's what I should do!"
said Kipper. But he wasn't very
good. He could only . . .

. . . wobble.

Some wrens had made a nest inside a flowerpot. It looked very cozy.

"I should sleep in one of those!" said Kipper. But Kipper would not fit inside a flowerpot.

He was much too big!

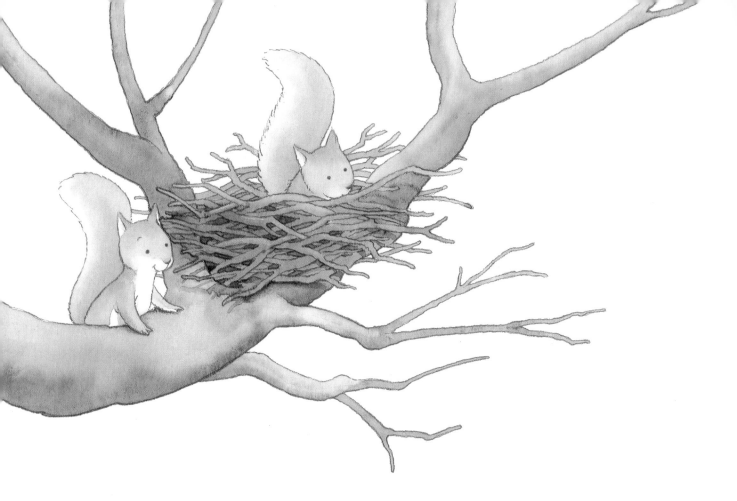

The squirrels had made their nest out of sticks.

"I will build myself a stick nest!" said Kipper. But Kipper's nest was not very good. He could only find . . .

. . . three sticks!

The sheep looked very happy
just sitting in the grass.
No, that was no good either.
The grass was much too . . .

. . . tickly!

The frog had found a sunny place in the middle of the pond. He was sitting on a lily pad.

"I wonder if I could do that," said Kipper.

But he couldn't!

"Perhaps a nice dark hole
would be good," thought Kipper.
"The rabbits seem to like them."

But it was not
a rabbit hole!

Kipper rushed indoors and hid
underneath his blanket—
his
        lovely
                old
                        smelly
                                blanket!

Kipper put the blanket back in his basket. He found his rabbit.

"Sorry, Rabbit," he said.

He found his bone and his ball.

"I like my basket just the way it is," yawned Kipper. He climbed in and pulled the blanket over his head.

"It's the best basket in the whole, wide . . ."

Sssssssssssshh

h h h h h h h !